TROLLS
United

TROLLS
United

Alan MacDonald
Illustrations by Mark Beech

BLOOMSBURY
CHILDREN'S
BOOKS

PRIDDLES: Roger, Jackie, and Warren
Description: Pasty-faced peeples
Likes: Peace and quiet
Dislikes: Trolls

MR. TROLL: Egbert / Eggy
Description : Tall, dark,
and scaresome
Likes: Roaring, tromping,
hiding under bridges

MRS. TROLL: Nora
Description: Gorgeous
(ask Mr. Troll)
Likes: Huggles and kisses,
caves, the dark

ULRIK TROLL
Description: Big for his age
Likes: Smells, singing,
rockball

GOAT
Description:
Strong-smelling,
beardy beast
Likes: Mountains, grass
Dislikes: Being eaten

To the children of
West Bridgford Junior School —A. M.

To my mum, Catherine —M. B.

Text copyright © 2007 by Alan MacDonald
Illustrations copyright © 2007 by Mark Beech

First published in Great Britain by Bloomsbury Publishing Plc
Published in the United States by Bloomsbury U.S.A. Children's Books
175 Fifth Avenue, New York, NY 10010
Distributed to the trade by Holtzbrinck Publishers

Library of Congress Cataloging-in-Publication Data
MacDonald, Alan.
Trolls united / by Alan MacDonald ; illustrations by Mark Beech. — 1st U.S. ed.
p.   cm.
Summary: Mr. Troll and Mr. Priddle bet on which of their sons
will make the school soccer team.
ISBN-13: 978-1-59990-125-1 • ISBN-10: 1-59990-125-0 (hardcover)
ISBN-13: 978-1-59990-126-8 • ISBN-10: 1-59990-126-9 (paperback)
[1. Trolls—Fiction. 2. Soccer—Fiction. 3. Fathers and sons—Fiction.]
I. Beech, Mark, ill. II. Title.
PZ7.M145Tu 2007   [Fic]—dc22   2007001444

First U.S. Edition 2007
Typeset by Polly Napper/Lobster Design
Printed in the U.S.A. by Quebecor World Fairfield
2 4 6 8 10 9 7 5 3 1 (hardcover)
2 4 6 8 10 9 7 5 3 1 (paperback)

Grump

THUMP, THUMP, THUMP! The sound of Ulrik kicking his new soccer ball against the wall echoed throughout the house.

"Look, Dad! Watch this!" cried Ulrik. The ball crashed against the wall, bounced onto the table, and landed neatly in Mr. Troll's bowl, spraying him with milk and Cocoa Puffs.

"Ulrik!" roared Mr. Troll. "Stop doing that!"

"Sorry, Dad. It was an accident. I've got to practice my shooting."

"Practice it somewhere else."

7

"Oh, Egbert, don't be such a grump! Let him play!" tutted Mrs. Troll. For the past few weeks her husband hadn't been himself at all. He did nothing but sit around the house all day watching television. Yesterday she'd found him with his nose pressed to the screen, chatting to someone on a talk show named *Oprah*.

She sat down at the table and emptied out a sockful of coins, stacking them into neat piles. Ulrik came to look over her shoulder.

"What are you doing, Mom?" he asked.

"Counting our peas[1]," said Mrs. Troll. "I've got to go shopping today."

"Are we rich?" asked Ulrik.

"I'm afraid not, my ugglesome. Everything costs a pile of peas. That's why I have to go out to work in the mornings."

"Humph! You call that work?" grunted Mr. Troll. "Delivering newspapers!"

"It's a good thing someone around here does

---

[1] Peas: pennies or money. Most trolls do not understand money. Offer them a nice rock or a thousand dollars and they will choose the rock.

some work," replied Mrs. Troll frostily. "If it was up to you, we'd all be living on Cocoa Puffs."

"I like Cocoa Puffs," said Ulrik. "But there are never any left. Dad eats them all."

"I do not!" protested Mr. Troll. He shook the bag only to find it was empty.

"Anyway," he said, changing the subject, "you're not the only one who can get a job."

Mrs. Troll stared at him. Ulrik stopped playing with the coins on the table.

"You got a job, Dad? Uggsome! What kind of job?" he asked.

"As a matter of fact, it's in a store," said Mr. Troll proudly.

"Eggy! That's wonderful!" exclaimed Mrs. Troll. "Why didn't you tell me before?"

"Well, I haven't gotten it yet."

"You just said you had!"

"No, I didn't," said Mr. Troll. "The interview's this afternoon. But once they meet me, they'll probably want to make me the boss of the whole store."

Ulrik and his mother exchanged looks. In the last month the Job Center had sent Mr. Troll on half a dozen interviews, but not one of them had been successful. Somehow he always returned home in a bad mood and refused to discuss what had happened.

"What kind of store is it, Dad?" asked Ulrik. "Do they sell soccer cleats?"

"They sell everything," said Mr. Troll. "It's that hulksome great store in town."

"Bagley's?" said Mrs. Troll. "Good goblins! You'd better change that undershirt."

"What's wrong with my undershirt?" asked Mr. Troll, inspecting the greasy stains on the one he was wearing.

"At least lick off the beans," said Mrs. Troll. "And when you get to the interview, don't go roaring—you know how it frights peeples. Just speak slowly and softly."

"Slowly and softly," repeated Mr. Troll.

"And be confident."

Mr. Troll nodded and scratched his enormous bottom in a confident manner.

Mrs. Troll glanced at the clock on the wall.

"Well, I must get to the store or there won't be any supper tonight. Are you ready for school, my hairling?" she asked Ulrik.

"Yes, Mom," said Ulrik.

"Let me see your fangs."

Ulrik bared the two small fangs on either side of his mouth.

"You haven't been cleaning them again, have you?" asked Mr. Troll.

"No, Dad."

"Or going in that shower?"

"No, Dad."

Ulrik tried to squirm away as his dad lifted his arms to sniff underneath. Only last week he'd caught Ulrik in the shower, dabbing himself with a bar of soap.

"Nice and stinksome," he said, satisfied.

Mrs. Troll planted a kiss on Ulrik's cheek and another on top of her husband's hairy head.

"See you later! Good luck with the interview, Eggy."

"I won't need luck," sniffed Mr. Troll.

Ulrik gave his dad a hug. "I hope you get the job, Dad. Can you get me some soccer cleats?"

Mr. Troll patted him on the head fondly. "Of course I will, my ugglesome. Leave it to me."

"We're going to have a soccer team at school," said Ulrik. "I've never been on a team before. Do you think I'll be good enough?"

"Good enough?" said Mr. Troll. "You're a troll, aren't you?"

"Yes, Dad."

"And what are trolls like?"

"Fierce and scaresome," said Ulrik, clenching his fists and baring his fangs.

"That's right!" said Mr. Troll.

"But Warren is good at soccer," said Ulrik.

"Huh! That porky kiddler next door? Have you ever heard Warren roar?" demanded Mr. Troll.

"No," admitted Ulrik.

"Because he can't. Let me hear you roar, Ulrik!"

Ulrik took a deep breath, puffed out his chest, and gave his best roar. "GRARGH!"

"Not bad," said Mr. Troll. "So if there are any soccer teams, who's going to be on them?"

"I am!" said Ulrik, and he thumped his soccer ball against the wall, bringing down the clock with a crash.

Robbers

MR. TROLL arrived at his interview almost an hour late. Bagley's was a large department store that spread over five floors, making it easy to get lost. He had spent a lot of time going up and down in an elevator. When he finally found his way to Mrs. Fussell's office on the fifth floor, it was almost four o'clock.

Mrs. Fussell was a small, silver-haired woman who peered at him over the top of her glasses. Mr. Troll wished he had a pair of glasses to peer over. He thought they would make him look important. When he was the boss of the store he would wear a different pair of glasses every day of the week.

"So, Mr. Troll," said Mrs. Fussell. "Tell me why you'd be suited to store work."

"Well," said Mr. Troll, "I'd be good at the roaring."

"The roaring?"

"Yes. Would you like to hear me roar?"

Mr. Troll stood up.

"Thank you, not just now," said Mrs. Fussell.

Mr. Troll sat down again.

"I'm afraid at Bagley's we don't really encourage . . . um . . . roaring," said Mrs. Fussell. "I would worry about scaring the customers."

"Ah, but it's not them I'd be frighting—it's the robbers," Mr. Troll explained.

Mrs. Fussell peered over her glasses at him. "The robbers?"

Mr. Troll wondered if she was a little deaf. She kept repeating everything he said. He spoke louder.

"Yes, ROBBERS that go about ROBBERING peeples."

"Please don't shout," said Mrs. Fussell. "If you

mean shoplifters, we have security guards to keep an eye out for them."

"I could keep two eyes out," said Mr. Troll. "I'd be good at that. I would hide so they wouldn't know I was there." He demonstrated how he would hide, squeezing his enormous body behind the filing cabinet in the corner.

"When I see them going about their robbering, I'd jump out and catch them red-handed. That's when I'd fright them with my roaring. 'GRARGH! GRARGH!'"

Mr. Troll roared so loud that the startled Mrs. Fussell almost fell off her chair.

"Mr. Troll," she said. "I wonder if you're really suited to store work. We're really looking for someone with experience."

"Oh, I've got experience," said Mr. Troll. "Buckets of it." He wasn't exactly sure what experience she meant, but he was doing his best to be confident. To emphasize his confidence, he placed his two hairy feet on the table and wiggled his toes.

Mrs. Fussell cleared her throat. "What kind of experience?" she asked. "Have you worked in a store before?"

"Well, not exactly," admitted Mr. Troll.

"Are you used to dealing with customers?"

"No."

"Then, do you know anything about clothes?"

"Not really," said Mr. Troll. "Where I come from, trolls don't wear clotheses. As a troggler I used to run around naked . . ."

"Yes, yes, I get the idea," said Mrs. Fussell hastily. She didn't really want to picture Mr. Troll running around naked; he was ugly enough with his clothes on.

"The thing is, I'd be good in a store," said Mr. Troll. "Just give me a try."

Mrs. Fussell prided herself on being a fair woman. Mr. Troll seemed so eager, the least she could do was give him a chance. She stood up.

"All right, let's see how you deal with people. Imagine I am a customer and you're serving me."

"You are a custard and I'm serving you," repeated Mr. Troll, getting to his feet eagerly.

"Now," said Mrs. Fussell. "Let's say I've come in with a complaint. I bought this jacket last week, but it's got a hole in the sleeve."

Mr. Troll looked bewildered. She was holding out her hands but there was nothing in them.

"Is it an invisible jacket?" he asked.

"No," said Mrs. Fussell. "Use your imagination. Pretend I've got a jacket."

"Ahh!" said Mr. Troll. He knew about pretending. At home, he often pretended to be a goblin while chasing Ulrik around the garden. He carefully took the pretend jacket off Mrs. Fussell and held it up to examine it.

"Nothing wrong with it," he said at last.

"What do you mean 'nothing wrong with it'? I just told you there's a hole in the sleeve!"

"No, there isn't," said Mr. Troll, smiling pleasantly.

"There is!"

"There isn't!"

Mrs. Fussell smoothed back a lock of hair. "Let's try again. I am the customer and I want you to replace this jacket with a new one."

"O-ho! Not on your bogles!" said Mr. Troll, wagging a fat finger. "I know what you're up to."

"I beg your pardon?"

"You're telling fib-woppers. Saying there's a holey sleevey just to get a new jacket."

Mrs. Fussell peered at him over her glasses. "So you refuse to exchange it?"

"Yes, I do," said Mr. Troll.

"In that case, I demand to see the manager."

"You can't," said Mr. Troll flatly.

"Why not?"

Mr. Troll spread his arms wide. "There aren't enough peeples! You're the pretend custard, I'm the pretend server—who's going to be the pretend manager?"

Mrs. Fussell gave up. "It is impossible," she thought to herself. "If Mr. Troll didn't scare off all the customers, he would certainly drive them all crazy."

"Let's just forget the jacket and sit down, shall we?" she said.

Mr. Troll sat down. "Did I get the job?" he asked hopefully.

"We'll let you know, okay?" said Mrs. Fussell. "Now, I still have a few more people to see. Did you complete the form we gave you?"

Mr. Troll's face fell. He had hoped she had forgotten about the form. He pulled a crumpled piece of paper from the pocket of his shorts. "This form?" he asked.

"That's right. Just leave your name, address, and telephone number."

Mr. Troll looked down at the form and then around the room, searching for some means of escape. The office suddenly felt much too hot.

"Do you need a pen?" asked Mrs. Fussell, handing him her own.

Mr. Troll took the pen and stared at the form again. Mrs. Fussell was waiting for him to write something, but he just gazed helplessly at the page. The words seemed to swim before his eyes like tadpoles.

"If you could hurry up," said Mrs. Fussell. "I do have other people to see."

Mr. Troll breathed in deeply and out again. He bunched his hands into two fists. Finally he stood up and, with a bellow like an enraged bull, tore the form into shreds that scattered on the carpet like confetti. Without another word, he stormed out of the office and slammed the door behind him.

On the label: Choccy bies.

Foul!

ULRIK walked up the neat gravel path and knocked on the Priddles' door. School was over for the day and he was eager to play with the new soccer ball he had tucked under his arm.

A plump, rosy-cheeked boy came to the door with a half-eaten chocolate cookie in his hand. Warren Priddle was in the same class at school and, ever since the Trolls had moved in next door, Ulrik had adopted him as a friend.

"Look, Warren," said Ulrik. "I've got a new soccer ball." He held up the ball. It was a little muddy, but then the Trolls' house was a little muddy too. Warren took the ball and bounced it twice.

"Should we play a game?" asked Ulrik.

"You don't know the rules," said Warren.

"I know some," said Ulrik. "I know you've got to kick a goal."

"Score," corrected Warren. "You 'score a goal.'"

"Okay, score a goal. Anyway, I've been practicing my scores against the wall," said Ulrik. "I'm going to be on the school team."

Warren let out a short laugh, which sprayed cookie crumbs over Ulrik. Half of the boys in his class wanted to be on the soccer team. Warren had told everyone he was sure to be picked as captain, but he'd never given a thought to Ulrik.

"Look," explained Warren, "I wouldn't get your hopes up. It'll only be the best players who are picked. Like me."

"What about me?" asked Ulrik. "I've never played on a team. And my dad's getting me some soccer cleats."

"Everyone's got soccer cleats," said Warren scornfully. "Anyway, I told you, you don't even know the rules."

"You could teach me," replied Ulrik. "We could play a game now."

Warren wiped his mouth with the back of his hand. As a rule, his mom didn't like the Trolls coming into the house. They dragged in dirt and leaves on their feet and left behind a strange smell. His mom said she doubted that they'd ever heard of deodorant. All the same, Ulrik didn't have to come into the house—they could play in the backyard. Come to think of it, Warren would take great pleasure in beating Ulrik at soccer.

Outside, Warren set up goals at either end of the lawn using some canes borrowed from his dad's vegetable patch.

"This is the goal," he explained. "You have to shoot the ball between these two posts."

"I know that," said Ulrik. "It's easy."

"Not when you're playing against me," said Warren, placing the ball in the middle of the pitch. "Ready? I'll be Italy. Who are you?"

Ulrik looked puzzled. "You know who I am."

"I mean, what soccer team are you?"

"Oh. I don't know any teams," said Ulrik. "Can I be Troll United?"

Warren rolled his eyes. "Okay. Troll United versus Italy. I'll kick off because it's my yard."

The game kicked off. Warren dribbled toward Ulrik, keeping the ball close to his feet. "This will be easy," he thought to himself. Although Ulrik was bigger, he was slow and clumsy and he wasn't wearing any sneakers on his big hairy feet. Added to that, he didn't have a clue how to play soccer. All Warren had to do was push the ball past him every time and he would win by a football score.

He stepped over the ball once or twice, showing off. Ulrik stood his ground, looking faintly puzzled—he thought the idea was to kick the ball, not dance with it. He waited until Warren got closer then—WHUMP!—he bowled him over with the force of a runaway train and came away with the ball. When he reached the goal, he thumped the ball between the two canes.

"Goal!" he shouted, with his arms in the air. "One point to me! Oh, Warren, are you okay?"

Warren was lying face down on the lawn where he had landed. He got to his knees and spat out a mouthful of grass. "Foul!" he said. "That was a foul."

"Sorry," said Ulrik. "I was only trying to tickle you."

"Tackle," said Warren, wiping mud off his nose. "You're too big and clumsy. You'll have to be more careful."

"Okay. I'll try," promised Ulrik. He knew he was a little clumsy. It came from having big feet and no soccer cleats. Warren placed the ball for a free kick and, after making Ulrik move back a long way, he scored.

"One zero to me!" he said, punching the air.

Ulrik went to get the ball from under the rose bushes. Soccer was turning out to be much more complicated than he had thought. It wasn't just a matter of tickling and scoring— there were other things called "fouls" and "free kicks" to worry about. He was already beginning to get confused with so many rules to remember.

Meanwhile, Mr. Troll had just returned from his interview. Hearing the thud of the ball against the backyard fence, he came outside to see what the noise was. He found his neighbor, Mr. Priddle, watching Ulrik and Warren chase a ball up and down the yard.

"I didn't know your Ulrik played soccer," said Mr. Priddle.

"Oh yes," said Mr. Troll. "He's going to play for the school team."

"That's funny," said Mr. Priddle. "Warren's been saying the same thing. I used to play a bit myself when I was his age. Just amateur stuff, of course, but I've got a few cups I could show you."

"I've got a teapot," said Mr. Troll, not to be outdone.

They watched Warren dribble around Ulrik and score another goal.

"See that?" said Mr. Priddle. "Warren's a natural. I was the same at that age."

"Covered in zits, you mean?" asked Mr. Troll.

"He isn't covered in zits," scowled Mr. Priddle. "He just has freckles. And I'll tell you something else, he's a better soccer player than your Ulrik."

"The bogles he is!" growled Mr. Troll.

"You want to bet on that?" challenged Mr. Priddle.

"Maybe I do," said Mr. Troll, sticking out his hairy chin.

"All right. Ten dollars says it's my Warren who gets picked for the school team!"

Mr. Troll bristled. "You mean my Ulrik *won't?*"

"Not a hope!"

"Oh no? We'll see about that!"

"It's a bet then. Let's shake on it." Mr. Priddle stuck his hand over the fence, and Mr. Troll grasped it and shook it so hard that his neighbor's teeth rattled.

Ulrik came over to see them, tired of picking the ball out of the roses.

"What are you talking about?" he asked.

"Nothing," said Mr. Troll. "Who won the game?"

"I did," said Warren, with a smug grin. "Thirteen to nothing."

Mr. Troll groaned and went back inside the house. Maybe he had been a little hasty to agree to the bet. He didn't know anything about soccer, and he didn't have any peas in his pocket because so far he'd failed to find a job. All the same, he was fed up with listening to Priddle boasting about his big-headed blubber of a son. It was time for Ulrik to show what trolls were made of.

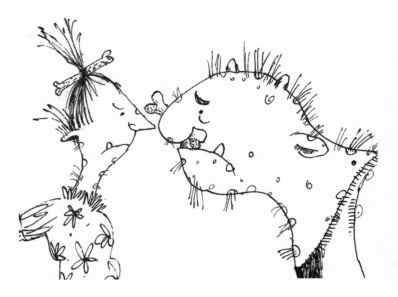

Scrawly Stuff

BACK home, Ulrik could hear raised voices in the kitchen. It sounded like his mom and dad were having an argument. This wasn't unusual—trolls will start an argument over nothing at all. Say "good morning" to a troll and he's quite likely to reply that it is a bad morning and what business have you got calling it good? This is really just to give him an excuse to roar at you. Mr. and Mrs. Troll were like any other married trolls, which is to say they argued and sulked all the time. Ulrik was so used to it, he paid little attention. But the argument he heard as he entered the kitchen sounded interesting, so he sat down on a chair to listen.

"I don't know why!" Mr. Troll was saying. "I just didn't get the job."

"But they must have given you a reason," said Mrs. Troll. "I bet you roared at them, didn't you? I warned you about that."

"I did not!" protested Mr. Troll. "I only roared once. Twice at the most."

Mrs. Troll sighed. "Did you remember to be confident, like I said?"

"I had confidence coming out of my ears," declared Mr. Troll. "I even put my feet on her desk."

"Oh, Eggy, you didn't!"

"What's wrong with that?" demanded Mr. Troll.

"You should have asked her first. Maybe *she* wanted to put her feet on the desk!"

"Oh, for bogles' sake!" said Mr. Troll, thumping his fist against a cupboard door.

Mrs. Troll shook her head. "You must be doing something wrong! You keep going for inter-views and getting turned down. There must be some reason."

"What do you mean by that?" demanded Mr. Troll huffily.

"I mean—there must be a reason!"

"You keep saying that!"

"Then just explain to me why you can't get a job!"

Mr. Troll's eyes bulged and he seemed to swell up like a great bullfrog. "The reason . . .," he said. "The reason, if you really want to know, is . . . oh . . . GRAARRGH!" He ended in a roar of frustration and stormed out of the room, slamming the door behind him.

Mrs. Troll sighed heavily and turned to Ulrik, who had been listening the whole time.

"Hello, my ugglesome," she said. "How was your day at school?"

"Okay," said Ulrik. "Did Dad get me the soccer cleats?"

"Oh, I'm sorry, hairling, I think he forgot. The interview didn't go so well."

"I heard," said Ulrik. "He didn't get the job."

"No," said Mrs. Troll. "I just wish I knew what he's doing wrong."

Ulrik nodded. He'd noticed his dad had been

grumpier than usual recently. Maybe there was something he could do to cheer him up.

Outside, he climbed the high green hill that took up most of the Trolls' yard. It was the only hill on Mountain View Street and could be seen

for miles around. Soon after they'd moved into Number 10, Mr. Troll had torn up the flower beds and replaced them with a pile of dirt. He missed the mountains and hills of his home in Norway. After dark, Ulrik sometimes scrambled up there on his own and sat under the stars. If he stared into the darkness long enough, he could imagine he was back on Troll Mountain looking out over the misty blue peaks and forests. He liked Biddlesden, but sometimes he felt a little homesick.

Reaching the top of the hill, he sat down next to his dad.

"Sorry you didn't get the job, Dad."

Mr. Troll grunted. "Huh! I didn't want it anyway. That store smelled funny."

"Never mind. You'll find another job," said Ulrik. "I brought you the paper."

He handed Mr. Troll the jobs page of the *Biddlesden Echo*. Mr. Troll spread it out on his lap and pretended to run his eye over the ads.

"What about the polices?" suggested Ulrik.

Mr. Troll knew about the polices—they'd been to his house more than once.

"Yes," he said. "I'd be good at that. Catching robbers and locking them up. I could drive one of those cars with a flashing blue nose."

Mr. Troll had come home in a police car the day he'd been arrested for lurking in a subway. It had made a deafening noise like a wailing troggler[2] and other cars had to pull over to get out of the way.

Ulrik pointed to an ad at the bottom of the page.

"What about this one? 'Taxi Driver Wanted. Must have own car.' "

"I don't have a car," said Mr. Troll.

"Oh—no," said Ulrik. "Still, there are lots of other jobs. Look at this one."

Mr. Troll snapped the newspaper shut abruptly. "I can't," he said.

"Dad, you didn't even read it!"

"No, Ulrik, you don't understand. I CAN'T."

"Why not?"

---

[2] A troggler: a baby troll. Troll babies wail almost continuously for the first six months of their lives. Parents give them to an old troll called a troggle-nurse, who is stone deaf.

"BECAUSE I CAN'T READ! I don't know how."

"Oh," said Ulrik. There was a silence.

"I never learned, you see," explained Mr. Troll. "When I growed up I didn't need to read or write. I was out chasing goats every day. But here it's all

different—'Get a job, earn some peas, write this, read that, fill in your name'—I can't do it, Ulrik. I haven't got a blunking clue."

"Is that why you didn't get the job in the store?" asked Ulrik.

Mr. Troll looked ashamed. "I ripped the form to

pieces. It's the same every time. I see all those black tadpoles on the page and it makes my brain boil. I can't help it!"

Ulrik laid his head on his dad's shoulder. He understood now why he came back from every interview in a foul mood. The truth was, Mr. Troll was embarrassed. He was a grown-up troll who couldn't write his own name. Ulrik had been at school for only a term and he could already write whole sentences in his notebook. "Yesterday, my dad threw a plate of bean at the wall" he had written only last week.

Suddenly an idea came to him.

"Why don't I help you, Dad? I know all my letters—I could teach you!"

Mr. Troll shook his head. "Thanks, my hairling, but it wouldn't work. I'm too old to learn now."

"No, you're not," said Ulrik. "Wait here!"

He scrambled down the hill and disappeared into the house. A minute later, he was back with a pencil and paper. He sat down and began to write, his tongue working with concentration. At last he handed the piece of paper to Mr. Troll.

Mr. Troll stared at the page blankly. "What's this?" he asked.

"Your name," smiled Ulrik. "EGBERT."

Mr. Troll marveled at Ulrik's handwriting. How had he managed to produce a son who was so smart? "This scrawly stuff is really me?" he asked.

"Yes, now you give it a try. Copy the letters."

"I can't!"

"It's easy, Dad. Just try!" said Ulrik.

Mr. Troll took the pencil. He spent a long time putting it on the paper and then drawing it back again, as if he thought it might burst into flames. Finally, he bent over the page and drew a wobbly line. After five minutes of painstaking labor he showed Ulrik what he'd written:

ƎƎGꓭƎЯP

"Okay! Good try," said Ulrik.

"It's wrong, isn't it?" said Mr. Troll staring at his writing hopelessly.

"Not all of it. The E's are backward and there are too many of them, but most of it's right."

Mr. Troll shook his head miserably. "I told you, I can't do it. It's a waste of time."

"No, it's not. You just need more practice. At school, we have reading and writing every day!"

"You do?"

"Of course."

Mr. Troll seemed very struck by this. For a long time he was silent, looking at the big wobbly letters he'd scrawled on the piece of paper. At last he stood up.

"All right," he said. "If kiddlers can learn to read, then so can I!"

"Uggsome!" said Ulrik. "I can bring home some of my books and help you after school."

Mr. Troll looked puzzled. "You won't need to," he said. "I'll be coming with you."

"With me? Where?"

"To school, of course. If I'm going to learn, I've got to do it properly—with real teachers and lessons."

Ulrik's mouth dropped open. "But, Dad . . ."

"Think of it," said Mr. Troll. "You and me in the same class—uggsome, eh?"

Ulrik was at a loss for words. His dad going to school? To *his* school? Was that such a great idea?

Two Times Troll

MRS. MELLY was dismayed to find a second troll in her class—it was bad enough having one. She hadn't forgotten that on his first day at school, Ulrik had bitten her. His dad looked like he could easily swallow her whole. He was sitting beside Ulrik now with his knees poking above the desk, like two hairy coconuts. The class was staring at him in open amazement. It had taken them a long time to get used to Ulrik, but Mr. Troll was another matter entirely. If he stood up, his head would almost make a dent in the ceiling.

"That's enough talking, Class 4," said Mrs. Melly. "I'd like you to get on with your work."

She walked among the desks, handing out a work sheet. Mr. Troll took one and stared at the rows of numbers in dismay. "Aren't we doing reading and writing?" he asked.

"Not this morning. On Tuesdays we start with math," said Mrs. Melly.

Mr. Troll waited till she'd gone and turned to Ulrik. "What are all these tadpoles?" he whispered.

"Shhh! It's math. You know, Dad. Add, subtract—it's easy!"

Mr. Troll looked blank. Subtract what? The work sheet might as well have been written in Ancient Egyptian. What did $+$ mean? Or $=$? He looked around the class and saw that all the children were busily working through the questions.

Ulrik seemed to be halfway through already.

"Move your arm," Mr. Troll whispered to him.

"What?"

"Ulrik, move your arm! I can't see the answers!"

Ulrik frowned at him. "Dad! You're not allowed to copy. You've got to figure it out for yourself."

Mr. Troll blew out his cheeks and slumped back in his chair. How could he figure out the answers when he didn't understand the questions? He checked to see that no one was watching him. Pretending to yawn he stretched out his arms, leaning over Ulrik's shoulder so that he could sneak a look at his paper.

"Mr. Troll!" said a stern voice behind him.

He swung around to see Mrs. Melly, who had apparently been standing at the back of the class the whole time.

"I hope you weren't copying," she said.

"Me?" said Mr. Troll.

"Yes, you! I saw you, looking over Ulrik's shoulder. Really, Mr. Troll, I'm surprised at you. I expected you to set a better example."

Mr. Troll hung his head. The other children were all gazing at him as if he had just robbed an old lady of all her peas. Mrs. Melly pointed to an empty desk by the window and told him to take his work over there. He did as he was told, dragging his big feet and grumbling to himself. School was turning out to be no fun at all. He could have been at home eating Cocoa Puffs and watching his favorite cartoon on TV.

At lunchtime, Ulrik lined up with his friends Josh and Alistair. It had been a long morning. His dad had hardly left his side for a moment. At break time, when he went out to play, his dad had tagged along. When they started a game of tag, he insisted on joining in.

Even when Ulrik went to the restroom, his dad followed him in and talked through the door. It wasn't that Ulrik minded exactly, but he could see that the other children thought it was strange. No one else had brought their dad to school. Then again, no one else had a dad who could reduce a class to tears just by poking his head around the door.

Ulrik studied the menu on the wall. He liked having school lunches. At home, they mostly ate cold bean straight from the can.

"Ulrik! Hey, Ulrik, wait for me!"

He turned to see his dad pushing his way through the lunch line. Ulrik sighed. He had been hoping for some time alone with his friends. He could tell they were getting a bit tired of his dad trailing after them all the time.

"I'm starving," announced Mr. Troll. "What's for lunch?"

Ulrik handed Egbert a tray from the pile. His dad raised it to his mouth and sank his fangs into it. "Ugh! Blech!" he said, spitting out a splinter of wood.

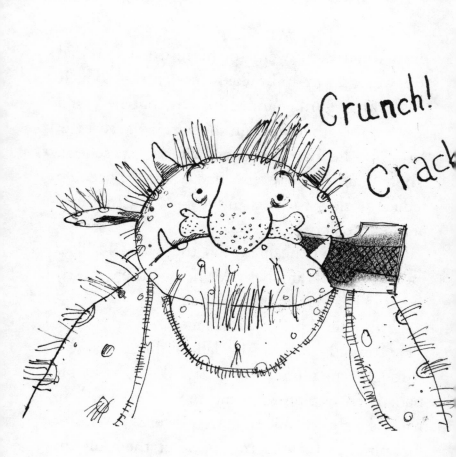

Crunch!

Crack

"It's a tray. You're not supposed to eat it," said Ulrik. "It's just for carrying your food." He did his best to explain the system for lunch, pointing to the serving lady, the menu, and the rack where the dirty plates were stacked. When he'd first started school, Ulrik had found lunchtimes confusing, and he could see his dad was puzzled by the whole idea.

The line had edged forward until they were in front of the serving lady. Ulrik knew the lunch ladies by now—his favorite was Mrs. Gibbs, who wore large, dangly earrings and greeted him in a friendly way. Mrs. Gibbs had never met his dad. When Mr. Troll's large, hairy head bent into view, she dropped her spoon into the gravy.

"It's all right," said Ulrik. "This is my dad. He won't hurt you."

Mr. Troll bared his fangs in a smile and prodded a tray of sausages wrapped in dough. "What's this?"

"Pigs in a blanket," replied Mrs. Gibbs. "Would you like some?"

Mr. Troll pulled a face. "Are they dead?"

"Dead?"

"These pigs. I don't want them jumping around in my bellies."

Ulrik nudged his dad's elbow. "They're not really pigs," he whispered. "They're sausages."

Mr. Troll peered into the tray as if he doubted this very much. "All right," he said. "Give me some pigs."

"Please," added Ulrik on his dad's behalf. A portion of food was spooned onto Mr. Troll's plate and returned to him. He stared down at the two sausages in dismay.

"Is that all?"

Mrs. Gibbs looked offended. "It's the same as everyone else gets. What vegetables do you want? Carrots or broccoli?"

Mr. Troll wrinkled his snout. "Trolls don't eat vegetables. They eat meat. This isn't enough to feed a hedgehog!" He pushed his plate back toward Mrs. Gibbs.

Ulrik glanced behind him. The line had come to a standstill, and people were starting to get impatient.

"Dad! Please!" he whispered. "Just take it and sit down. You're holding everyone up!"

They found a table in the middle of the hall. Ulrik sat between Josh and Alistair, while Mr. Troll took a seat opposite them. He was still staring down sulkily at the two lonely sausages on his plate. Ulrik decided it was best to ignore him.

"Have you seen the sign?" Josh was saying excitedly. "It's on Thursday, after school."

"What is?" asked Ulrik.

"The tryout game—what do you think? You've got to sign up if you want to play."

Ulrik paused with a carrot halfway to his mouth. He hadn't known the tryouts were going to take place so soon. Although he'd been practicing every day, he wasn't sure he was ready yet. He didn't even have a pair of soccer cleats to wear.

"'Scuse me," his dad interrupted, "but are you eating that pig?" He pointed to the remaining sausage on Josh's plate.

"Um, sorry . . . I am," said Josh.

"Oh," said Mr. Troll, disappointed. Ulrik could see his dad's plate was already empty and he was looking around the dining room in search of something else to fill his empty stomach.

"Why don't you go and ask if there are any seconds, Dad?" he suggested.

"Seconds?" said Mr. Troll. "Are they vegetables?"

"No, second helpings," explained Ulrik. "There might be some more sausages."

"Really?" said Mr. Troll eagerly. "I can have as many as I want?"

Ulrik shrugged. "As long as there's plenty left over. You just have to ask."

He glanced back at the serving lady and saw there were only a few children now in line. Mr. Troll set off with his empty plate, evidently cheered by the prospect of more food. At home he could easily work his way through six cans of bean by himself, noisily licking out the can when it was empty. The child-size portions served at school were no match for a troll with his appetite.

Ulrik went back to the conversation.

"You really think we could get on the team?" he asked.

"Why not?" said Josh. "We've got as much chance as anyone else."

"That's not what Warren thinks. He told me not to get my hopes up."

"Huh! Warren! I wouldn't listen to him," said Josh scornfully. "He has such a big head."

"Does he?" said Ulrik. He tried to picture Warren's head. It *was* quite big, when you thought about it.

"Anyway," said Josh. "It's Mr. Wigg who decides. He's coaching the team."

Before Ulrik could reply, they were interrupted by the return of Mr. Troll. He was carrying a bucket, which he set down on the table with a heavy thud.

"You were right," he said. "There's plenty of seconds. No one seems to want them."

Ulrik stared in surprise. The bucket was filled to the brim with pieces of sausage, jam, carrots, and cold rice pudding—all mixed together in a sludgy mess. Slowly it dawned on him what it was.

"Dad! No!" he shouted. "Don't eat that . . ."

But it was too late. Mr. Troll had already plunged his spoon into the slop bucket and was raising it to his lips. He slurped down a mouthful noisily.

"Mmm, not bad," he said, offering them the bucket. "Anyone want some seconds?"

Alistair turned away. "Ugh! I think I'm going to be sick."

Ulrik realized the dining room was silent. Everyone had stopped eating. They were all watching Mr. Troll in disbelief, as one spoonful after another disappeared into his mouth. A splotch of rice pudding escaped his tongue and dribbled down his chin, falling onto the table. Mr. Troll wiped it up and sucked his finger.

"You know, Ulrik, we should try this at home," he said.

Ulrik buried his face in his hands. It was only the first day and already his dad had managed to embarrass him in front of the whole school.

Size Elevens

THANKFULLY, the rest of the afternoon passed without further disaster.
During English, Mr. Troll practiced writing his
own name over and over again while the rest of
the class wrote a story. When he got home, he
flopped into an armchair and flicked on the TV,
declaring that all this learning had exhausted
him.

Ulrik went to find his mom to tell her about the
soccer tryouts on Thursday. To his delight, she
agreed to take him into town then and there to

look for some soccer cleats. He had never owned a pair of cleats before, and he was very excited about it. Somehow he imagined that they would magically transform him into a better soccer player. Scoring goals would come easily. He would be able to pass, dribble, tickle, and do that juggling thing where you kept the ball in the air.

"Now, you're sure this is what you want?" his mom asked when they reached Bagley's Department Store.

"Yes, Mom!" said Ulrik impatiently. "Everyone has soccer cleats. All my friends have got them."

"Yes, but remember, you're not used to them. You may find cleats uncomfortable."

"I won't!" promised Ulrik.

They went inside. The sports department was on the third floor. Ulrik enjoyed riding the escalator while Mrs. Troll held on tight to the handrail and jumped off at the top, afraid that she might be sucked down the crack where the steps were disappearing. Ulrik ran on ahead, stopping to stare at pool tables, tennis rackets, skis, and snowboards. He had never been in a sports store before.

"Look at this, Mom!" he pointed. "A running machine."

"Don't be ridiculous, Ulrik. There's no such thing. Machines can't run."

"This one does. Can we see it work?"

Ulrik stepped onto the treadmill. Nothing happened. He pressed a red button and the machine hummed into life, with lights flashing on the panel. Suddenly, the floor beneath his feet began to move backward at high speed. Ulrik shot backward, landing in a heap among a display of golf clubs.

"Whoa!" he said. "That was fun. Can I do it again?"

"Excuse me, can I help you?" asked a young sales assistant, turning off the treadmill.

"Oh, yes," said Mrs. Troll. "My son needs some cleats for school."

"Soccer cleats," added Ulrik, getting up. "I'm going to play for the school team."

The sales assistant nodded. "Okay." She spoke in a bored, singsong voice as if having to talk tired her out. They followed her to the footwear department.

Ulrik gazed at the rows and rows of soccer cleats on display.

"Uggsome!" he said.

"What size is he?" asked the assistant.

"Well, he's growing so big," said Mrs. Troll. "Almost up to my chest."

"No, I mean what shoe size?"

"Oh, I don't know. He's never worn shoes before."

"Right." The assistant regarded the trolls as if they were plainly out of their minds.

"My dad says shoeses are for softies," explained Ulrik. "Trolls don't need them because we've got hard, horny feet." He lifted his right foot to show the assistant the tough leathery skin on the bottom.

"We'll try a size seven," she said.

Ulrik tried on a pair of black cleats that he liked the look of, but he couldn't squeeze his foot inside—even when he lay on his back and pulled with all his might.

"Have you got something a bit bigger?" asked Mrs. Troll.

"Not in children's," said the assistant. "That's the largest pair. He'll have to try an adult's."

Ulrik spotted a shoe in silver leather and took it down to admire it.

"Look at these, Mom. They're all shiny—can I try them on?"

The assistant came and went, bringing different sizes of shoes and rolling her eyes when Ulrik said they were too small. Finally, they found a size 11 shoe that fitted him snugly.

"Walk around in them," urged Mrs. Troll. "I don't want you getting them home and saying they pinch your claws."

Ulrik walked up and down. He tried running in the cleats. It felt good. He imagined he was playing for the school team and swung his foot at an imaginary ball. "Goal!" he shouted, punching the air. A rack of sandals behind him toppled over and crashed to the floor.

"Okay, we'll take those," said Mrs. Troll hurriedly. She reached into her bag and brought out a sock. "How many peas?"

"Peas?" The sales assistant blinked.

"You know, *peas*. Fifty peas, ninety peas."

"Oh, I see." The assistant checked the tag on the box. "They're $59.99," she said. "I'll put them in a box for you."

Mrs. Troll's mouth dropped open. Fifty-nine

dollars? For one pair of soccer cleats? It would take her weeks to earn that much! She emptied out the sock on the store counter and a shower of coins spilled everywhere, some rolling off the counter and onto the floor.

"Is something the matter?" asked the assistant.

"No, no. I've just got to count these," said Mrs. Troll, picking up pennies from the floor.

Ulrik bent down to help. People in the store were staring at them.

"Eight dollars, thirty-two peas," said Mrs. Troll at last. "That's not enough, is it?"

The assistant shook her head. "I can take a credit card."

"What about some rice pudding?" Mrs. Troll offered a can from her bag, but the assistant looked at her coldly and began to pack the cleats back in their box.

Mrs. Troll looked at Ulrik. "Sorry, hairling, we don't have enough peas."

Ulrik's face fell. "But Mom, the tryout's on Thursday. I'll be the only one without cleats!"

Mrs. Troll sighed and turned back to the shop assistant. "Haven't you got anything cheaper?" she said. "Please. There must be something."

"For eight dollars?"

"Yes."

The assistant rolled her eyes and pointed at a rack to her left. "Only those. They're $7.99."

"What are those?"

"Wellington boots."

"They're for playing soccer?" persisted Mrs. Troll.

The assistant shrugged, pushing out her lower lip. "Guess so. You can do what you like in them."

Mrs. Troll went over to the rack and selected a pair of bright red Wellingtons, which she held out to Ulrik. "What do you think, Ulrik? These are stylish! Why don't you try them on?"

Ulrik sat down and reluctantly pulled on the boots. He didn't want them. They weren't like soccer cleats at all. They were made of a soft, flubbery material, and they came up to his knees. When he walked, they flapped around and made a sound like wet fish.

"They don't have knobbly parts," he grumbled. "They're supposed to have knobbly parts on the bottom."

"We can give them knobbly parts," said Mrs. Troll. "Don't worry about that."

Ulrik stared down at his feet miserably. He wanted the silver shoes, but he knew that even if he waited for weeks, his mom would never be able to afford them. In any case, the tryouts were on Thursday and he needed something to wear. It was the red Wellingtons or nothing. He looked up at his mom's hopeful face.

"Well?" she asked. "Should we take them?"

Goats

THE next morning, Ulrik found his new boots sitting at the end of his bed. When he picked them up, he was surprised to find studs stuck to the soles. They weren't the usual kind of studs you get on most cleats. These were fashioned out of plastic bottle caps stuck on with a generous amount of glue. His mom must have worked on them while he was asleep. Ulrik felt a little guilty for sulking all the way home from the store the day before. He tried on the boots. The bottle caps made a strange crunching noise underfoot. Since they were different sizes he found he walked unevenly, rolling from side to side, as if he was on the deck of a ship.

"How are the boots?" His mom smiled brightly when he came down to breakfast.

"Oh, they're . . . um . . . good," said Ulrik. "Thanks, Mom."

"Why don't you take them to school? You can try them out."

"Okay," said Ulrik. He squashed the boots into his school bag, pushing them down well out of sight.

At break time, he went in search of Mr. Wigg's sign and found it pinned on the board outside the school office. There were already eighteen names on the list, and Ulrik added his own under Josh's.

"I was wondering when you were going to sign up," a voice said behind him. He turned and almost bumped into Warren Priddle.

"Not long now," said Warren. "I hope you've been practicing."

"I have," said Ulrik. He rubbed his snout awkwardly. "Actually, there's something I wanted to ask you."

"Want me to explain offside again?" asked Warren.

"It's not that," said Ulrik. "It's these." He pulled out the red boots from his bag and held them out for Warren to inspect. A grin spread slowly over Warren's face.

"Nice boots," he said.

"Are they?"

"Oh yeah, these are cool, Ulrik."

Ulrik looked surprised. "I was going to wear them for the tryout game," he said. "What do you think?"

Warren blinked at him. "You mean to play soccer?"

"Yes. Why—are they the wrong kind?"

Warren seemed to be having some trouble with his mouth, which was twitching upward at the corners. He got it under control.

"No, no," he said. "They're great. Seriously, these are great boots."

"Really?"

"Are you joking? Red Wellingtons! I think Brazil plays in these."

"Brazil? Is he good?" asked Ulrik.

"He? It's only the best team in the world."

"Wow!" said Ulrik. "So it's okay to wear them tomorrow?"

"Of course! Wear those and you're bound to make the team."

"You really think so?"

"Trust me," said Warren, with a sly grin.

"Okay. Thanks, Warren!"

"No problem."

Ulrik put the boots in his bag and headed back to his classroom, feeling greatly relieved. For some reason he had been anxious about showing the boots to Warren. He had even imagined Warren might make fun of his bottle-cap studs. But it turned out he didn't have to worry—the boots were fine. Better than fine. With boots like that, he was bound to make the team.

Ulrik had been so worried about the new boots that he'd almost forgotten about his dad. He found Mr. Troll waiting for him in the classroom.

"Where did you go at break?" he demanded. "I've been looking for you everywhere."

Mrs. Melly clapped her hands and waited for the

class to pay attention. She announced that they were going to have Circle Time. Ulrik normally enjoyed Circle Time, as it was a chance for everyone in the class to talk about anything they wanted.

"So," said Mrs. Melly, "who has something they'd like to tell the class?"

Ulrik raised his hand, eager to talk about his new boots. But next to him, his dad's hand stretched highest of all.

"Yes, Mr. Troll. As it's your first week, what would you like to tell us?" asked Mrs. Melly.

Mr. Troll rose from his seat. "I would like to tell about Norway. Norway is where trolls live."

"Yes, we know that," said Mrs. Melly. "Perhaps you can tell us something about Norway? I'm sure it must be very different from Biddlesden."

"Very different," said Mr. Troll. "Biddlesden is tiddly-piddly country. Norway is big." He stretched his hands wide apart. "Big mountains, big forests—big as a goblin's nose." He looked at the class. Having explained the bigness of Norway, he wasn't sure how to go on.

Katie Morris raised her hand. "Are there other trolls like you?" she asked.

"Hundreds," said Mr. Troll. "Trolls live high in the mountains where peeples never come. Peeples in Norway are frighted by trolls. They make up bad stories about us. They think we're going to eat them."

"But you wouldn't, would you?" said Katie, eyeing Mr. Troll's fangs a little uncertainly.

"Blech, no!" said Mr. Troll, poking out his tongue. "Peeples taste bad. They smell like soap. What trolls like to eat is goat."

"Ugh!" said Nisha.

Mr. Troll eyed her sternly. "Have you ever eaten goat pie? It's the most tastesome thing in the world. Better than bean any day of the year." An idea came to him and his eyes lit up. "Shall I show you how a troll catches a goat?"

Everyone in the class nodded eagerly. This sounded far more interesting than Circle Time. Ulrik could see that his dad had gotten the class's attention, though he wasn't so sure that a lesson in goat hunting was such a good idea. Mr. Troll tended to get a bit carried away whenever he talked about his favorite subject.

"Say I'm tromping along through the forest one morning, minding my own business," he began. He walked up and down, stamping his feet and humming a song to himself. Suddenly, he stopped and got down on all fours, sniffing the ground like a dog. "Then I smell something," he said. "The stinksome smell of a goat!"

Everyone in the class leaned forward, almost as if they each expected a goat might trot into view at any moment. Mr. Troll cast his eyes around the room for someone to help.

"Mrs. Melly," he pointed. "You be the goat."

"Oh, no, I'd rather not," replied the teacher. "Perhaps one of the students . . ."

"Too small!" replied Mr. Troll impatiently. "I'm not after kiddlers. This is a big ninny-goat I'm catching!"

Mrs. Melly wasn't sure it was a compliment to be compared to a ninny-goat, but Mr. Troll had her by the arm and was already pulling her into the middle of the circle.

"What do you want me to do?" she asked.

"Be a goat," said Mr. Troll. He poked two fingers above his head as if they were horns. "You know—goat. *Trot trot, bah baahh!*"

Feeling rather foolish, Mrs. Melly took a few steps forward. "Bah!" she said.

Mr. Troll gave her a pitying look as if this was the most unconvincing goat he'd ever heard. The students, however, were beginning to enjoy themselves. They'd never heard Mrs. Melly do animal impressions before.

"Now," said Mr. Troll. "I can try to catch this goat, but goatses run faster than trolls, so what shall I do?"

"Dig a hole," suggested Alistair.

"Hide!" suggested Nisha.

Mr. Troll nodded. "Hide! Exactly! Now you are thinking like a troll."

He began to rearrange the furniture, dragging a table into the middle of the circle. On either side of it he placed two chairs, forming steps up to the table.

"What's he doing now?" Josh whispered to Ulrik.

"Making a bridge," said Ulrik. He had a feeling he knew what was coming next, and he was pretty sure that Mrs. Melly wouldn't like it.

"Sooner or later, goatses always cross rivers," Mr. Troll was saying. "*Trip trop, trip trop* they go over a bridge. And that's where a clever troll hides, down in the danksome dark."

He crawled under the table on his hands and knees to wait for a passing goat. Only his hairy head could be seen poking out.

"Listen," he said, with a hand to his ear. "I hear a ninny-goat coming!"

Mrs. Melly hesitated. No one had warned her she'd have to climb on tables. She didn't have much of a head for heights. But the students were all looking at her expectantly, and it was a bit late now to put a stop to Mr. Troll's hunting lesson. She stepped on the first chair a little unsteadily.

"Bahh!" Mr. Troll reminded her, from under the bridge.

"Bahh!" replied Mrs. Melly, setting one foot on the table.

This was the moment Mr. Troll had been waiting for. He sprang out from his hiding place and swung himself up onto the table, landing with such force that it shook like a leaf. Drawing

himself up to his full height, he bared his fangs and let out an earsplitting, bloodcurdling roar. "GRARRRRRRGH!"

If Mrs. Melly had been a goat, she would have turned and fled. But goats are more sure-footed than teachers. She took a step back in alarm, and her foot missed the edge of the table. There was a moment when she seemed to be practicing the backstroke in midair, then she tumbled backward and disappeared from sight.

Ulrik closed his eyes, hardly daring to look.

When he opened them again, his dad was holding a pale-looking Mrs. Melly in his arms. He set her down on a chair as the class burst into applause.

"And that," he said with a bow, "is how a troll catches a goat."

Mrs. Melly didn't reappear after break. The principal said she had gone home to lie down and recover. Ulrik had a feeling that they wouldn't be having Circle Time again for a while.

That evening, Ulrik climbed the hill in the backyard. It was his favorite place when he wanted to be by himself and think. The sky was growing dark, and the first stars were coming out in the sky. On the far horizon, he could see the hills that always reminded him of home. Footsteps approached and a hand touched him gently on the shoulder.

"Come on, my ugglesome—time for bed," said his mom.

"Not yet," pleaded Ulrik. "Can't I just stay out a bit longer?"

Mrs. Troll sat down beside him and slid an arm around his shoulders.

"Thinking of home?"

"Yes," said Ulrik. "I miss it sometimes—our stinksome old cave."

"I know," said Mrs. Troll. "I miss it too."

They sat in comfortable silence for a while, thinking about home and the friends they'd left behind.

"How were the boots?" asked Mrs. Troll at last.

"Oh, they're great," said Ulrik. "Warren says Brazil has boots like that."

"Brazil, eh? Is that good?"

"Brazil is the best in the world, Mom."

"There you go—I told you they'd be okay. And how was school today?"

"Okay," said Ulrik.

"I mean, how is it working out with your dad?"

"Oh, that." Ulrik studied the grass between his feet.

"He hasn't been getting into trouble, has he?" asked Mrs. Troll.

"Well, not that much trouble."

Mrs. Troll sighed. "I thought so. I hope he didn't go roaring at the kiddlers?"

"Oh, no," said Ulrik. "He only roared at Mrs. Melly, and she was being a goat."

He could tell he would have to explain the whole thing from the beginning. He told her about the goat hunting and Mrs. Melly's scare on the bridge. None of it was really his dad's fault, Ulrik explained; it was just that school was still new to him.

"But, Mom," he said. "I was thinking . . ."

"Yes?"

"How long's it going to last—Dad coming to my school?"

Mrs. Troll glanced up at the darkening sky. "I don't know, my ugglesome. I only wish I did."

Temper, Temper

AS far as Ulrik could see, his dad had forgotten all about getting a job. He was enjoying himself far too much at school. It turned out that he was "a natural learner," as he told anyone who would listen. He couldn't imagine why he hadn't started school before—he had no idea he would be so good at it. The walls of the kitchen were covered in his pictures—pictures that said GOAT or CAR in his large, wobbly handwriting. During mealtimes he fell into a habit of spelling out words in conversation, which after a while got rather annoying. "Pass the M-I-L-K," he would say. Or, "Are we having B-E-A-N for supper?"

On Wednesday, Ulrik checked the list on the bulletin board again. It had grown to twenty-one names, including his own. He had been working on his soccer skills in the yard every evening, but it was boring practicing alone. He needed someone to help him. After school he went to find his dad, who was in the living room, hunched over a picture book called *The Three Little Pigs*.

"Dad, can you help me practice my soccer?" asked Ulrik.

"Not now, Ulrik," said Mr. Troll. "I've got homework to do."

"But, Dad, it's the tryout tomorrow. You haven't seen me play in my new boots."

Ulrik proudly showed off the red Wellingtons on his feet. Mr. Troll closed his book with a sigh. He was just getting to the good part—when the little piggies get eaten.

Outside, Ulrik set up a goal at the bottom of the yard.

"You be the goalkeeper," he explained. "You've got to stop me from scoring."

"That's easy," said Mr. Troll.

He wrestled Ulrik to the ground and in a few moments was sitting on top of him.

"Let's see you score now," he said, tickling him under the arms.

"No, Dad—ha ha!—get off!" giggled Ulrik. "That's not how you play soccer. You're not allowed to fight me."

"No fighting?" said Mr. Troll. "What kind of game is that?[3]"

He climbed off Ulrik and helped him to his feet. It seemed pointless to him. Where was the fun in a game if you couldn't sit on your opponent?

Ulrik placed the ball, while Mr. Troll went back to stand at his goal.

"Ready?" asked Ulrik.

---

[3] Trolls' favorite game is rockball, in which two teams try to gain possession of a rock in a forest. Biting, kicking, and wrestling are permitted. The game ends when both teams admit they have lost the rock and a draw is declared.

"Ready," said Mr. Troll.

Ulrik ran up and thumped the ball as hard as he could. It sliced off the toe of his boot and rose high to the left. At the last moment, Mr. Troll stuck out a large fist and swatted it away as easily as a fly.

"Wow!" said Ulrik. "Great save! You're an uggsome goalie, Dad!"

"Am I?" said Mr. Troll, looking pleased with himself.

Ulrik grabbed the ball and tried again. This time he kept his shot low, but Mr. Troll simply stuck out a foot and hoofed it away. After a dozen shots, Ulrik had only managed a single goal.

"Maybe you're not doing it right," suggested Mr. Troll.

"It's these boots," complained Ulrik. "I keep slipping on the grass."

"Then take them off," said Mr. Troll. "Boots are for babies!"

"But everyone wears soccer cleats, Dad. I won't be on the team if I don't have cleats."

"Of course you'll be on the team," said Mr. Troll. "It's just a matter of confidence. What am I always telling you?"

Ulrik thought hard. "To stay out of the shower."

"Besides that."

Ulrik thought again. "I'm too gentle for a troll," he said.

"Exactly. You've got to get angry, Ulrik. Lose your temper."

Ulrik frowned. How could he lose his temper when he wasn't sure he had one to lose?

"Where does your roar come from?" asked Mr. Troll.

Ulrik shrugged. "From my mouth."

"Wrong," replied Mr. Troll. "A troll's roar comes from his bellies. You've got to find your roar inside you, Ulrik. It starts deep down and comes rumbling up, like a belly burp."

"And will that get me on the school team?" asked Ulrik.

"Of course it will," said Mr. Troll. "Now, I'm going inside. When I come back, I want to hear a roar that will scare the pants off me."

As the sun sank lower in the sky, Ulrik ran up and down the hill, practicing his roar. He tried to think about it coming from deep down in his belly, but that only made him hungry. A smell of cooking was coming from the kitchen, where Mrs. Troll was preparing supper.

Next door, a curtain twitched at an upstairs window, where two figures stood watching.

"What's he doing now?" asked Mr. Priddle.

"Search me," said Warren. "Shouting at the trees. Whatever it is, it's not soccer."

"You're sure he won't make the team?" asked Mr. Priddle.

"Ulrik? He doesn't have a clue," said Warren scornfully.

"Good. I don't want to lose my bet with old Hairy Face next door. And remember, I'll double your allowance if we win."

"Don't worry, Dad. It's in the bag," said Warren. "See what he's got on his feet?"

Mr. Priddle pressed his nose against the window to look closer. "Hard to tell. They look like boots—Wellington boots."

Warren grinned. "They are."

"Why is he wearing those?"

"Because he thinks they're for soccer."

Mr. Priddle shook his head, baffled. "He must be crazy. You can't play soccer in Wellington boots!"

Warren bared his teeth in a sly grin. "Exactly."

The truth of this dawned on Mr. Priddle, who was sometimes a bit slow on the uptake.

"Poor old Ulrik!" he said, chuckling to himself. "Poor old Ulrik!"

Tryouts

ULRIK pulled on his socks, trying to ignore the nervous gurgling of his stomach. In a few minutes, the game would be starting. He was wearing his best red T-shirt and a pair of shorts that were a little on the small side. Looking around the classroom, he noticed that everyone else had real soccer clothes in the colors of their favorite teams. Warren Priddle had a large number nine on the back of his Italy shirt, and his name in capital letters. He was kneeling down to lace up his cleats.

Ulrik reached into his bag and took out the red Wellingtons. He sat on the floor to pull them on.

Josh paused from fiddling with goalkeeper's gloves to look at him.

"What the heck are those?"

"My boots."

Josh frowned and then broke into a grin. "Good one! I thought you were serious for a minute!"

"I am," said Ulrik, standing up. "These studs feel a bit funny."

He stamped his feet to make sure the boots were on properly.

"Ulrik!" said Josh. "You're not *really* going to wear those!"

"Why not?" Ulrik looked around. He saw Warren nudging Ryan. The two of them were darting looks in his direction and snickering with their heads together.

Mr. Wigg came into the room with a soccer ball tucked under his arm. His bald head shone like a billiard ball under the lights.

"Everyone changed?" he said.

"I am, Mr. Wigg," smirked Ryan. "But I think you should take a look at Ulrik."

Mr. Wigg stood by Ulrik and stared down at him. By now, the other players were crowding around to see what was going on. Ulrik rubbed his snout. He wished everyone would stop staring.

"What's all this, Ulrik?" said Mr. Wigg.

"My new boots, sir."

"I can see that. Where are your soccer cleats?"

"These are soccer cleats, sir."

"Don't be silly—they're Wellingtons, Ulrik. This is soccer—we're not going for a walk in the country!" There were hoots of laughter, with Warren's high-pitched giggle rising above all the rest. Ulrik felt his face glowing. He was starting to feel like he'd made a mistake.

"Quiet!" barked Mr. Wigg. He lowered his voice, bending down to speak more kindly. "Haven't you got anything else, son? What about your sneakers?"

Ulrik shook his head miserably. "I don't have any."

"Well, you'll just have to do the best you can then. Lucky for you, it's raining outside. You can splash in the puddles."

The players ran out onto the field, and Ulrik brought up the rear in his big, flapping boots.

He glanced toward the sideline where his dad

stood watching. Mr. Troll waved and then pulled a scowling face to remind him that trolls were fierce and scaresome.

Mr. Wigg raised a whistle to his mouth and blew to start the game. For a long time Ulrik didn't touch the ball, but he ran up and down a great deal while his dad gave him useful advice from the sideline.

"Get him, Ulrik! Tromp on him! Grab him by the ears!"

He was playing in midfield, but he wasn't quite sure where that was. He tried to find someone on his team who looked like a midfielder, but it was difficult to tell. The red boots flapped and squeaked as he ran, slowing him down. The rain fell steadily, and soon they were all caked in mud. Two of the bottle caps had come off so that he ran in a strange, lopsided way, and he sometimes lost his balance altogether.

Warren had the ball and was racing toward the penalty area. A moment later, the ball flew past Josh's outstretched hand and high into the net. Mr. Wigg paused to write Warren's name in his notebook.

Ulrik always seemed to be too late to reach the ball. When he ran upfield, the ball would be booted over his head toward the other end. And when he ran back, the ball would zip past him going the other way. He knew he wasn't doing enough to impress Mr. Wigg and get in his notebook. But just before halftime, he found himself in the right place for once. The ball bounced in his own penalty area, and Ulrik got to it before Warren could pounce to score. "Move, Ulrik!" shouted Josh, coming out of the goal. Facing his own goal, Ulrik swung his foot, intending to launch the ball into the sky. But what he launched was his right boot. It flew off and struck Josh on the nose.

"Owww!" yelled Josh, going down in the mud.

"Sorry, Josh!" said Ulrik.

"Goal!" cried Warren, tucking the ball away into the net.

Mr. Wigg blew his whistle and ran over to check that Josh wasn't seriously hurt. He had gotten to his feet, but his nose was the color of an overripe plum.

"It's all right—nothing broken," said Mr. Wigg.

"Sorry, Josh," said Ulrik again. "It's these boots. They won't stay on."

Josh felt his nose. "You're dangerous. You could have taken my head off!"

Mr. Wigg suggested that Josh come out of the game for a while, until he was feeling better. Josh peeled off his gloves, but after what had happened, no one seemed eager to risk playing goalie.

"Come on," said Mr. Wigg impatiently. "We can't start the game without a goalkeeper."

"I could do it," said an eager voice from behind the goal. "I'm an uggsome goalie."

It was almost five o'clock when Mr. Troll and Ulrik finally got home. Mrs. Troll was waiting for them expectantly. In Ulrik's honor she had cooked his favorite meal—a bean and banana pie, which she was just taking out of the oven. She looked up as Mr. Troll burst through the door, followed by Ulrik—both of them covered in mud from head to toe.

"Hello, my hairlings!" said Mrs. Troll. "How did your soccer go?"

"Oh, not so well," replied Ulrik in a hollow voice.

"It was uggsome!" said Mr. Troll. "You should have been there. I was amazing."

Mrs. Troll looked puzzled. "You, Eggy? I thought you were only going to watch."

"I was!" said Mr. Troll. "But then Ulrik's team was losing, wasn't it, Ulrik?"

"Two to nothing," said Ulrik gloomily.

"And no one wanted to go in goal. So I said I didn't mind going in and . . . guess what? It turns out I'm the best goalkeeper in the school!"

"Really?" said Mrs. Troll dryly.

"Dad was great," said Ulrik. "He saved everything. Mr. Wigg wants him on the team on Saturday."

"Imagine that!" said Mr. Troll. "Me on the school team!"

"Imagine!" said Mrs. Troll, glaring at him. She turned to Ulrik. "And what about you, my ugglesome? Are you on the team too?"

Ulrik shook his head. "I'm just the reserve."

"The reserve? Well! That sounds important," said Mrs. Troll.

"It's not," replied Ulrik, pulling off his muddy boots and throwing them into a corner. "It just means you sit on a bench and watch. Warren says nobody wants to be the reserve."

Mrs. Troll sighed. She knew how much Ulrik had been looking forward to playing for the school team. He had been practicing for weeks. It didn't seem fair.

"Never mind," she said. "Sit down and have some supper. I've made your favorite, Ulrik."

"I'm starving," said Mr. Troll, reaching over to cut himself a thick slice of pie. "Playing goalie makes you hungry. You'll have to come and watch me on Saturday. Think of it, me on the school team!"

He broke off. Ulrik had pushed away his plate with the pie untouched.

"What's the matter, hairling?" asked Mrs. Troll.

"I'm not really hungry. I think I'll just play in my room."

He trudged upstairs, and they heard the door of his bedroom click shut.

Mrs. Troll turned to glare at her husband.

"How could you, Egbert! See how you've upset him!"

"Me?" said Mr. Troll through a mouthful of pie. "What did I do? You're the one who made him wear blunking boots!"

"He wanted them!" said Mrs. Troll. "He's been begging me all week!"

"Well, a fat lump of help they were," said Mr. Troll. "He played like a ninny-goat on ice. Galumphing around and bashing peeples' noses!"

Mrs. Troll stood up and squared her shoulders. "Well, at least I'm trying to help," she said. "Not like some trolls I could mention."

"What do you mean by that?" bristled Mr. Troll.

"If you'd gotten a job, I could have bought him the right shoes!"

Mr. Troll got to his feet. "Oh, it's my fault, is it?"

"Yes, it is!"

"Well, we'll see about that!" said Mr. Troll, picking up his plate. A second later the plate hit the wall, with beans and pieces of banana splattering the floor. Mr. Troll stormed out of the room.

"Where do you think you're going now?" shouted Mrs. Troll.

"To get some blunking soccer cleats!" replied Mr. Troll as he slammed the front door.

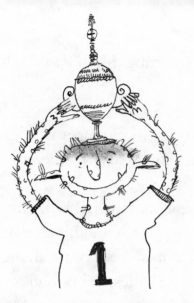

The Big Match

S ATURDAY, the day of the big game, finally arrived. Ulrik couldn't help getting his hopes up. "Maybe someone won't show up," he said on the way to the school. "Then Mr. Wigg will have to put me on the team." Mrs. Troll didn't answer. She had worries of her own. After last night's argument, Mr. Troll had failed to return home. It was pretty normal for him to storm out of the house sulking, but Mrs. Troll had never known him to be gone a whole night. She had hardly slept a wink.

"You're not listening, Mom!" said Ulrik, tugging at her arm.

"What?"

"I said, 'Is Dad going to meet us there?'"

"Oh, I expect so, my ugglesome. He didn't say."

When they reached the school, the two teams were already out on the field, practicing at either end. A small crowd had come along to watch, including the Priddles, who had come to see Warren. But there was no trace of Mr. Troll.

Mr. Wigg hurried over to meet them.

"Where's your dad, Ulrik? It's nearly time for kickoff!"

"I don't know," said Ulrik.

"We were hoping he might be here," said Mrs. Troll worriedly. "I hope nothing's happened to him."

Ulrik pointed past her shoulder. "It's okay, Mom. Here he comes now!"

Mr. Troll was striding across the field toward them, in the company of two police officers. Ulrik recognized them as the same pair who had arrested Mr. Troll once before.

Mrs. Troll threw her arms around her husband.

"Eggy! Where on earth have you been?"

"We found him in Bagley's, madam, trying to steal a pair of cleats," said the policeman.

"I wasn't stealing," said Mr. Troll indignantly. "I just wanted to borrow them."

"We've been over this," said the policewoman wearily. "You can't borrow things from a store window. When you break the glass, it sets off the alarm."

"Oh, Eggy, you didn't!" said Mrs. Troll.

Mr. Troll rubbed a bump on his forehead sheepishly. "It was an accident!" he said.

"And why didn't you come home?" asked Mrs. Troll. "I've been out of my mind with worry."

Mr. Troll explained he had spent the night at the station. The police had asked him a lot of questions, after which they had given him a nice room of his own with a bed. The sergeant had even locked the door so that he would feel safe.

"Have you got to sleep there tonight?" Ulrik asked.

"No," said the policewoman. "Luckily for you, Mr. Bagley has agreed to drop the charges."

"Who's Mr. Bagley?" asked Mrs. Troll.

"Very important peeples," Mr. Troll informed her. "Mr. Bagley is the big boss at Bagley's. He wants to see me on Monday morning."

"Oh dear!" sighed Mrs. Troll.

"Anyway," said the policeman, "we'll be getting

back to the station. Looks like you've got a match to play." He smiled at Ulrik. "Nice boots. What position are you playing?"

Ulrik hung his head. "I'm just the reserve. But Dad's playing goalie."

"Goalie? He's a bit old for that, isn't he?"

Mr. Troll looked offended. "I'm an uggsome goalie," he informed them. "You should stay and watch me make some savings."

The opposing team stared in astonishment as a huge, hairy troll bounded across the pitch to take up his position in the goal. Mr. Troll's head grazed the crossbar, and when he crouched in the goal, it almost disappeared from view.

The teacher from Dewberry School tried to object. "You can't play him," he grumbled. "He's practically a giant!"

"Actually, he's a troll," said Mr. Wigg. "And it's not his fault if he's big."

Mr. Troll smiled at the teacher, baring the two sharp fangs on either side of his mouth. That seemed to settle the matter. The teacher decided he had better find his whistle and start the game.

The match kicked off—Biddlesden in red shirts playing against Dewberry in all-white.

"Come on, Biddlesden!" cried the supporters on the sideline.

"Go on, Eggy!" cried Mrs. Troll excitedly.

It soon became clear, however, that Biddlesden was in for a hard game. The Dewberry team was quicker to the ball and stronger in the tackle. They passed the ball swiftly from player to player so that Biddlesden hardly got a kick.

"Don't stand there! Stomp on them!" Mr. Troll bellowed to his defense. After only a few minutes, he was called into action. From a corner the ball was kicked high into the penalty area, and several of the Dewberry players ran in, ready to head it home.

"I've got it!" roared Mr. Troll, and players on both sides scattered as he came charging out of his goal. In his excitement he lost sight of the ball, but he found it again when it struck him on the head and bounced away to safety.

"Well done, Eggy!" cheered Mrs. Troll.

"Great save, Dad!" called Ulrik.

Mr. Priddle shook his head. "He's supposed to

catch the ball, not head it," he grumbled. But Mr. Troll had his own approach to playing goalie. As Dewberry took control of the match and launched one attack after another, only Biddlesden's hairy number one kept them in the game. Shots rained in from every angle, but Mr. Troll somehow kept them out. The ball bounced off his knee, thumped into his belly, and cannoned off his legs to safety. Once, when he stopped to watch an ambulance pass by, a shot took him by surprise and struck him on the bottom.

At the other end of the field, his team took advantage of its luck. On a rare attack, a long shot from Warren took a lucky bounce in the mud and skidded past the goalie. One-nothing Biddlesden.

On the sideline, Ulrik cheered with everyone else. He wanted his school to win, but he dearly wished he was out on the field taking part. For the last half hour he had been running up and down, trying to keep warm in the biting wind. Whenever the ball went off the field he ran to get it, hoping that Mr. Wigg would notice and be impressed.

When the halftime whistle blew, Biddlesden was still ahead and hanging on by a thread. Ulrik listened hopefully as Mr. Wigg gave his halftime speech. Surely it would be his turn in the second half? But Mr. Wigg didn't mention his name or even glance in his direction. He walked away feeling miserable.

As he put his gloves back on, Mr. Troll felt a hand on his arm.

"Eggy!" said Mrs. Troll. "Look over there."

Mr. Troll turned and, for the first time, noticed Ulrik on the sideline. He was sitting all by himself, hugging his knees to his chest to try and stop himself shivering.

"What's the matter with him?" asked Mr. Troll. "We're winning!"

Mrs. Troll stared at him. "Winning? Winning? You really don't have a clue, do you?" She stalked off in a huff.

Mr. Troll furrowed his brow. He'd been so caught up in the game, he hadn't given much thought to Ulrik. But it was obvious, even to him, that something was wrong. Things started to come back to him from the last few weeks. He remembered Ulrik asking him for a pair of soccer cleats—shoes that he'd failed to get him. He remembered Ulrik practicing every day, thumping his ball against the dining room wall. He recalled the crestfallen look on Ulrik's face when he wasn't picked for the team. It finally dawned on him—some fat lump had stolen Ulrik's place on the team—and the fat lump was *him*!

"I'm a big useless," he muttered to himself. "The biggest useless in the world."

The game restarted but a few minutes into the second half, disaster struck. Mr. Troll came rushing out of his goal to clear a ball from his penalty area. No one saw what happened, but the next moment he had collapsed in a moaning heap. The ball bounced on and rolled very gently into the empty goal. Dewberry had tied the game and there was worse to come. When Mr. Troll tried to get to his feet he sat down heavily, clutching his foot.

Mr. Wigg came running onto the field, followed by Ulrik and Mrs. Troll.

"Eggy, are you all right?" she asked, kneeling beside him.

"Argh! Ohh!" groaned Mr. Troll. "I think I've sprained my uncle."

"Don't you mean your ankle?" said Mr. Priddle.

"Whatever it is, it hurts!" replied Mr. Troll, scowling.

He was helped off the field, supported by Mrs. Troll and Mr. Priddle and groaning with every step.

"What a pity!" said Mr. Wigg regretfully. "And just when he was playing so well."

He turned to Ulrik. "Ulrik, you'll have to go in. Josh can play goalie—you play in defense. And please try not to injure anyone."

"Yes, Mr. Wigg," said Ulrik, already peeling off his jacket.

Mr. Troll sat down on the sideline. "Don't worry about me," he said with a wink. "You get out there. What are trolls?"

"Fierce and scaresome," replied Ulrik.

"Don't forget it. Oh, and one other thing."

"What?"

"Those boots. Maybe you'd play better without them."

Ulrik looked down at the red Wellingtons. Maybe his dad was right. He pulled them off and ran onto the field in his bare feet to applause from the small crowd of supporters. His stomach felt like it was tied in knots. He tried to remember the advice his dad had given him, but it seemed to have gone from his head.

It felt like years before he got a chance at the ball, and when he did he hurried his pass, which went to the other team. He saw Warren shake his head and turn away in disgust. Biddlesden was under pressure, and without Mr. Troll, it seemed only a matter of time before they would let in another goal. When a clever pass slipped through the defense, Ulrik found himself racing for the ball with the tall, redheaded number nine.

"Stop him, Ulrik!" called Mr. Troll.

"Boot it out!" cried Josh.

Ulrik was about to kick the ball out for a throw, when number nine lunged in hard with his studs.

"Owww!" cried Ulrik, holding his foot and hopping around.

"Oooh!" cried the crowd.

"Foul!" protested Mrs. Troll. But the referee was the Dewberry teacher, and he waved them to play on. Looking up, Ulrik saw number nine with the goal at his mercy, steadying himself to shoot. At that moment, Ulrik felt something rumbling up inside him: a roar that rose from deep in his belly and came out of his mouth, like the angry growl of a bear.

Number nine saw Ulrik coming and yelped, leaping high in the air to avoid the tackle. Ulrik swiped the ball and rampaged upfield. In

seconds, he was over the halfway line. The white-shirted players made no attempt to tackle him—they'd never seen a troll with a temper before, and it seemed wiser to get out of the way. To his left, Ulrik could hear Warren urging him to pass—but he kept going until he was bearing down on the goal, with only the nervous-looking goalie in his way. He took aim and let the ball fly.

It flew like a missile toward the top corner. The goalkeeper made a despairing dive and got his fingertips on it, but it made no difference. The net shivered and a great cheer went up.

Ulrik stood blinking in amazement, wondering what had come over him.

On the sideline, Mrs. Troll grabbed Mr. Priddle in a bear hug that lifted him off the ground. Minutes later the final whistle blew, and Mr. Troll bounded out to hoist Ulrik onto his shoulders and carry him off the field in triumph.

"Funny," remarked Mr. Priddle to his wife. "A moment ago he could hardly walk."

Mrs. Priddle clicked her tongue. "Well, I hope that will teach you to make silly bets, Roger. Don't say I didn't warn you."

Mr. Priddle reluctantly took out his wallet and drew out a ten-dollar bill. Half of it, he decided, would be coming out of Warren's allowance.

Job for a Troll

THE following Saturday, Ulrik found himself once again outside Bagley's Department Store with his mom.

"You're sure he said to meet him here?" asked Mrs. Troll.

"Yes, I told you."

"But why? What's this all about?"

Ulrik shrugged. "He wouldn't say. He just said to come to the store."

Mrs. Troll smoothed down her best floral dress. Ever since her husband had been to see Mr.

Bagley on Monday morning, he had been acting very mysteriously. He had stopped going to school, but every morning he left the house early and returned home at six o'clock, with a secretive smile on his face. He wouldn't tell them where he went, even though Ulrik tried to get it out of him by tickling his feet. "Wait and see," Mr. Troll had said. "Just wait and see."

Inside, the store was so crowded that it was hard to move without bumping into someone. Ulrik wrinkled his snout at the strong smell of perfume coming from one of the counters. His mom flopped down on a nearby sofa.

"This is hopeless!" she said. "We'll never find him in all these peeples."

"GRARRGH!" A burly figure leaped out from behind a chest of drawers, making them both jump. Mr. Troll burst out laughing at the surprised look on their faces.

"Dad!" said Ulrik. "You frighted me!"

"I did, didn't I?" said Mr. Troll, looking pleased with himself. "I've been watching you ever since you came in. If you were a robber, I'd have caught you red-handled."

Mrs. Troll stared at her husband. He was wearing a dressy brown jacket, with a peaked cap perched on the back of his hairy head.

"What's this?" she asked.

"My uniform," said Mr. Troll, showing it off proudly. "See, it's even got my name on the badge. Egbert Troll—Security Guard. Egbert with two E's."

"You mean—you work here, Dad?" said Ulrik, greatly impressed.

"That's right, Ulrik. I have to keep my eyes out for robbers and shopsniffers."

"Wow! And what if you see one?"

"I chase them through the shop and sit on their bellies till the polices arrive."

"So that's where you've been sneaking off to every morning," said Mrs. Troll.

"I told you I'd get a job," said Mr. Troll.

"And you were right, my clever old snuggler," said Mrs. Troll, kissing her husband on the tip of his snout.

Mr. Troll took them on a tour of the store. On

the way, he explained that it had been Mr. Bagley who had offered him the job. The last security guard had taken early retirement, as he was getting too old to chase shoplifters down the street. Mr. Bagley said he needed someone big and fearless, and Mr. Troll fit the bill perfectly.

"Well, I'd better get back to work," he said, at last. "You never know when one of these shop-sniffers might be trying to rob something."

By the door, he paused. "Oh, Ulrik, wait a minute. I got something for you."

Mr. Troll reached under a counter and brought out a slim white box.

"What is it?" asked Ulrik.

"Open it and see."

Ulrik took off the lid and peeled back the layers of tissue paper. Inside was a pair of shiny silver soccer cleats.

"I hope they're okay," said Mr. Troll, smiling bashfully.

Ulrik's eyes shone. "Okay?" he said. "They're uggsome!"

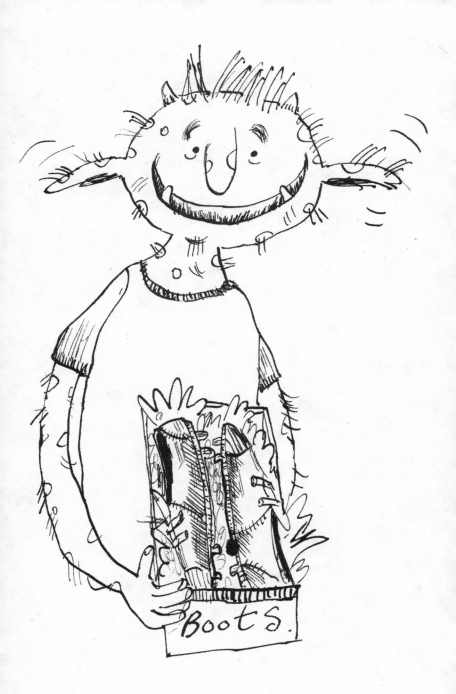

ALAN MACDONALD has written and directed plays for children and has written for the BBC. He is the author of several children's books, including *Wilfred to the Rescue* and *The Pig in a Wig*. He lives in England.

MARK BEECH divides his time between illustrating children's books and working as a commercial artist in the world of advertising and product development. He lives in London, England.